THE LAND of THIS and THAT

For Ms. Chic, with gratitude

NEITHER

Airlie Anderson

LB

LITTLE, BROWN AND COMPANY

NEW YORK   BOSTON

Once upon a time, there were two kinds:

this

and **that,**

these

and **those,**

one or the **other**.

Until . . .

I'm from the Land of **This** and **That**, but I'm Neither. So I'm looking for Somewhere Else to fit in.

This isn't Somewhere Else, but you will fit in here.

Where is here?

Excuse us. We're from the Land of **This** and **That**, but we don't fit in at home. We are looking for Somewhere Else.

Well, this isn't Somewhere Else. This is the Land of All. And **everyone** fits in here.

Once upon a time, there were many kinds:

this   and   that,

somewhat   and   **whatnot,**

either,   very,

sort of,

just,

rather,

a little,

neither and both....

And all were

welcome!

Author's Note

I love the practice of drawing and painting: the feeling of brush-on-paper, the way it sharpens my noticing skills. It made me start to notice in-between moments, the beautiful in-between-ness of things, which is what *Neither* is about. I began sketching this little creature in a coffee shop, where all my favorite ideas start. Once I had enough doodles and words—they come at the same time—I brought my sketchbook into the studio, where I drafted many miniature versions of the book with a pencil and several (!) erasers. For the finished paintings, I used gouache (opaque watercolor) on hot press watercolor paper.

—Airlie Anderson

This book was edited by Deirdre Jones and designed by Jen Keenan. The production was supervised by Virginia Lawther, and the production editor was Marisa Finkelstein. The text was set in Clichee, and the display type is hand-lettered.

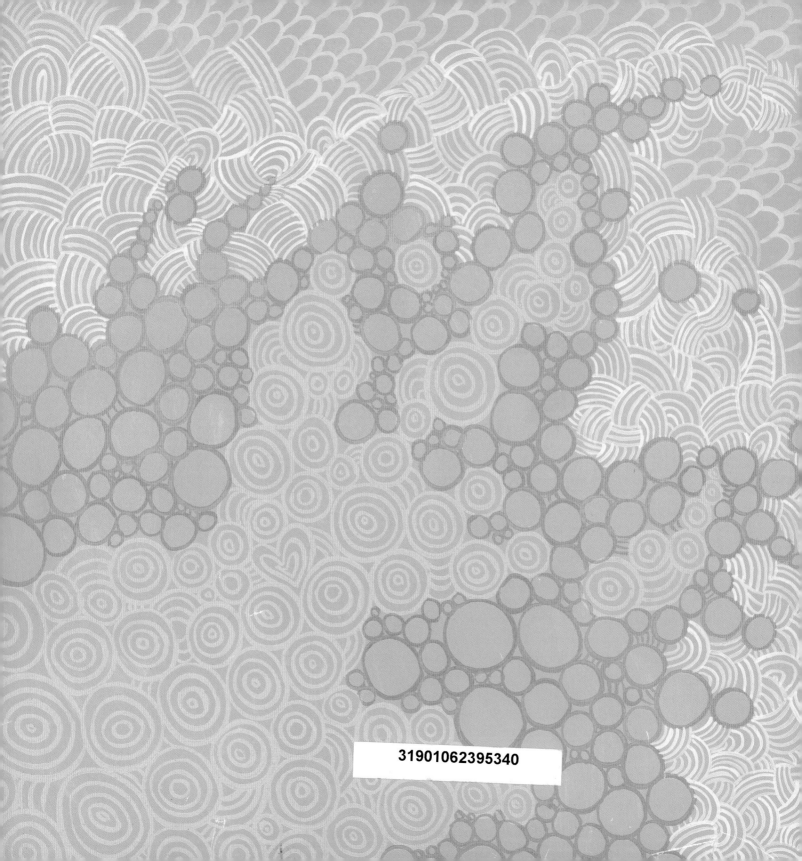